KT-155-302

This LADYBIRD TALE
belongs to

....

The Magic Porridge Pot

Retold by Vera Southgate M.A., B.COM
with illustrations by Marcin Piwowarski

LADYBIRD 🐞 TALES

ONCE UPON A TIME there was a little girl who lived with her mother, who was a widow. They were so poor that one day they found they had nothing left to eat.

The little girl went off into the woods to play. She was so hungry that she began to cry. An old woman came up to her.

"Why are you crying, my child?" she asked.

"Because I am so hungry," said the little girl.

"Then you shall be hungry no more," said the old woman. She gave the little girl a small cooking pot.

Then the old woman said, "When you are hungry, just say to the pot, 'Cook, little pot, cook!' It will cook some very good porridge for you."

"When you want the pot to stop cooking," went on the old woman, "you must say, 'Stop, little pot, stop!'"

The little girl was so hungry that she wanted some porridge at once. So she said to the little pot, "Cook, little pot, cook!"

The little cooking pot did as it was told, and began to cook some porridge. The little girl could hardly wait to try some.

When the porridge was cooked, the little girl said, "Stop, little pot, stop!" The porridge tasted very good and the little girl ate every little bit of it.

The little girl ran home with the cooking pot to her mother, and told her what the old woman had said.

"Now our worries are over," said her mother happily. "The little pot will keep us well fed!"

Whenever they were hungry, they said to the cooking pot, "Cook, little pot, cook!"

The porridge was always very good, and they always enjoyed it.

One day the little girl went out for a walk. While she was out, her mother felt hungry. So she said, "Cook, little pot, cook!"

The pot began to cook some porridge. The mother began to eat it. It was very good porridge and she enjoyed it.

She was so busy eating the porridge that she forgot to tell the pot to stop cooking.

The pot went on and on, cooking more and more porridge.

Soon the porridge began to come over the top of the little cooking pot.

When the mother saw this, she knew that she must tell the pot to stop cooking. But she had forgotten the words!

The pot just went on and on, cooking more porridge. Soon there was porridge all over the table and all over the kitchen floor.

And still the little pot went on, cooking more and more porridge!

Soon all the house was full
of porridge.

And still the little pot went on,
cooking more and more porridge!

Soon the house next door was full of porridge.

And still the little pot went on, cooking more and more porridge!

Soon all the houses in the street were full of porridge.

And still the little pot went on, cooking more and more porridge!

Soon nearly all the streets in the town were full of porridge.

And still the little pot went on, cooking more and more porridge!

All the people, from all the houses, came out into the streets.

No one knew how to stop the little pot from cooking more porridge. It just went on and on, cooking more and more porridge.

The people in the town began to think that soon all the world would be filled with porridge.

Just as the porridge was reaching the last house in the town, the little girl came back from her walk.

At first, she could not tell what had happened to the town.

"Please stop the little pot from cooking any more porridge," cried her mother.

The little girl said, "Stop, little pot, stop!"

And then, at last, the little pot did stop cooking porridge.

But anyone who wants to go into that town now, will have to eat his way through a lot of porridge!

A History of
The Magic Porridge Pot

The Magic Porridge Pot remains a much-loved fairy tale today. Its success is arguably due to its simple rhythm and rhyme, and its popularity as a children's nursery story.

The story of *The Magic Porridge Pot* as we know it today was recorded in *Children's and Household Tales* by the Brothers Grimm, in the 19th century. There are many similar tales in existence around the world, including the Indian story of the pan that cooked endless amounts of rice when a single grain of rice was placed in it.

Ladybird's 1971 classic retelling of the story by Vera Southgate has contributed to the lasting popularity of the tale.

Collect more fantastic
LADYBIRD 🐞 TALES

Little Red
Riding Hood

9781409311126

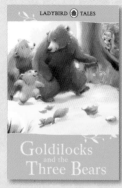

Goldilocks
and the
Three Bears

9781409311119

Cinderella

9781409311072

Jack
and the
Beanstalk

9781409311102

The
Gingerbread
Man

9781409311096

The Three
Little Pigs

9781409311089

The Three Billy
Goats Gruff

9781409311065

Hansel
and
Gretel

9781409311133

Puss in Boots

9781409311225

Rapunzel

9781409311195

Rumpelstiltskin

9781409311164

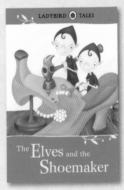

The Elves and the Shoemaker

9781409311188

Snow White and the Seven Dwarfs

9781409311171

The Enormous Turnip

9781409311218

The Magic Porridge Pot

9781409311201

Sleeping Beauty

9781409311157

Endpapers taken from series 606d,
first published in 1964

A catalogue record for this book is available from the British Library

Published by Penguin Random House Children's UK: One Embassy Gardens,
8 Viaduct Gardens, London SW11 7BW
A Penguin Company

007

© Ladybird Books Ltd MMXII

LADYBIRD and the device of a Ladybird are trademarks of Ladybird Books Ltd

All rights reserved. No part of this publication may be reproduced,
stored in a retrieval system, or transmitted in any form or by any means,
electronic, mechanical, photocopying, recording or otherwise,
without the prior consent of the copyright owner.

ISBN: 978-1-40931-120-1

Printed in China